My Date With Bubble Tea

Sylvia Morrow

COVER CREDITS

Cover Artist Anastasia Novikova
Cover Designed by Unfortunate Reads

CONTENT NOTES

Talk of finances, unusual genitalia, explicit descriptions of sexual encounters, sex saves the day trope, descriptions of food, being grossed out by something unexpected during a consensual sexual experience.

ABOUT THE SENTIENT OBJECT HOLIDAY SERIES

The Sentient Object Holiday Series is a shared series of stories written by some of your favorite off-the-wall authors: Biblio Barbie, Dakota Cockaday, Holly Wilde, Luna Cantrip, Nicole Parker, Sylvia Morrow, Thea Masen, Unfortunate Reads, and Vera Valentine. It is meant for readers 18 and over ready to embrace a deeper experience with some unusual holidays. Find the collection on Amazon.

CHAPTER ONE
Adanna

"Who's my good girl? Who's my sweet little powder puff? Yes, you are! My cute little Snappy-Snap!"

I tickle my Pomeranian under her furry little chin as she sits comfortably in her baby carriage. She got tired on our walk through the park, so I've put her somewhere to lounge while I enjoy the rest of this sunny late afternoon. Her pink tongue rolls out as she smiles her doggy smile. She's a bit pampered, but everyone deserves a little luxury.

"Alright, you're strapped in tight. Let's go find the doggy park so you can see the other puppies!" Before moving on, I take my phone out of my purse and snap a few pictures of her for my story. People will just eat these up. "There. Now we can go!"

Strolling along in the beautiful May weather has put me in such a wonderful mood. It'll be fantastic to take Snappy out to play. I look forward to watching her frolic with the other tiny dogs. Nothing could distract me from my destination.

...except for that exceptionally gorgeous man sitting on the bench. *Wow.*

I nearly stumble when I see him. Sitting under the shade of the trees, he's sipping a bubble tea, one of my favorite drinks. The gentle wind is ruffling his wavy, asymmetrically cut, black hair. His cheeks are rosy against his pale skin, making him look like he could be college age, though the crinkles around his eyes say he has to be closer to my age of thirty-four. His lean body stretches out when he yawns and I take in every inch of it, including the tiny sliver of skin that shows when his t-shirt rides up.

Shit. I'm staring. Okay, I need to keep walking or make a move, not just stand here like a creep. *Come on, woman up, Adanna.*

He tucks the hand not holding his tea into the pocket of his navy-blue cardigan and relaxes back onto the bench, a smile quirking a corner of his lips as he stares off into the distance. The ease of that smile, how it sits there like his default expression, intrigues me. I've been around too many men with permanent scowls—being with someone who knows how to smile could be a nice change. *Yeah, I've got to talk to this guy. Hopefully, he's into weird dog ladies.*

I square my shoulders and exhale before pushing Snappy toward the bench. *Here goes nothing.*

Before I can make it there, however, something goes very wrong.

The man disappears with a *poof*.

All that's left on the bench is an extra-extra-large bubble tea, and hovering over it is a shocked-looking fairy.

CHAPTER TWO
Adanna

"Oh dear. That wasn't supposed to happen," the fairy squeals.

The baby carriage stops next to the bench, bumping softly into it. I realize I've kept on walking through my amazement. My brain had been scared stiff, but my feet didn't get the same message.

The fairy startles at my disturbance of the crime scene, only now becoming aware of my presence. Her mouth opens in a shocked O before she flies down to the bench to stand in front of the overly large bubble tea. She's only about a foot and a half tall, with translucent, opalescent wings, but it's clear she's doing her best to block the view of the two-foot-tall, plastic cup of tea.

"Oh, hello. Don't mind me. Nothing to see here," she says with a nervous laugh. She gestures down the path with her sparkly wand. "Enjoy your walk! Have a lovely day!"

"Nothing to see? You've gotta be kidding me. I'm looking at a real fairy," I say as I sit next to her on the bench. "Not to mention the fact that there was definitely something to see a minute ago when you turned an entire man into a drink. A really handsome man, by the way. What happened? What are you gonna do?"

"Heh. About that." The fairy looks side to side with another nervous laugh, her purple hair starting to come loose from her messy bun. Her voice lowers to the point I can barely hear it. "I don't know what to do in this situation."

"What do you mean you don't know what to do? You can't leave him like that." I wave my arms indignantly in his direction.

I was planning on trying to date him, Miss Fairy!

"Well, that wasn't supposed to happen. Oh, I think I'll have to call for backup." The fairy jumps into the air and waves her wand in several glittering circles. "Mrs. Petunia, I need you!"

With a *pop*, *another fairy appears, and this one is* larger all around. If the gray hair and wrinkles are any indication, she's also older.

"What is it, Miss Dandelion?" She turns to me and her green eyes grow wide. "And why is there a human with you?"

The fairy who must be Miss Dandelion clutches her wand tightly, her tiny hands twisting nervously back and forth around it.

"Oh, well, I was turning the stubborn caterpillars into chrysalises when I sneezed. My magic accidentally hit a man holding a drink. Now the man *is* the drink, and I can't seem to turn him back into a man. The lady and the dog just happened to be there."

Snappy yips, happy to be acknowledged.

"Oh my. I've never had a case of an accidental *drinkening* before," Mrs. Petunia says as she inspects the bubble tea.

Suddenly, the lid on the plastic cup begins to flap up and down. I nearly jump out of my skin when a voice comes out.

"Happy to be your first," it says wryly.

"Snappy! That drink just talked!" I shriek.

"Aren't you observant," the tea replies.

"No need to be rude," I snap back.

The tea chuckles, his ice cubes clinking along.

"Hmm. I have a thought. The woman was here when he was changed, correct Miss Dandelion?" Mrs. Petunia asks, tapping her wand on her chin as she paces back and forth. "And she came right over to ask about him?"

Miss Dandelion nods.

"This reminds me of a routine true love's kiss fate case I had in the past. With a more unusual twist, of course," Mrs. Petunia twirls her wand for no particular purpose, still thinking.

"An unusual twist." Miss Dandelion nods.

"Also, more extreme. This is no simple Princess and frog-type scenario." Mrs. Petunia stops walking to stare at me.

Miss Dandelion joins the other fairy in staring. My head swivels between the two of them.

"Why are you staring at me?"

"The more severe the transformation, the further you have to go for the solution," Miss Dandelion says with a sigh.

"Dear, you're going to have to take him home." Mrs. Petunia flies over to the bench next to me and takes a seat, placing her little hand over mine. She looks up at me with a solemn expression. "I believe you're the only one who can save him."

"Why me? And how am I supposed to do that?"

Anxiety gurgles in my stomach.

"You're obviously here for a reason. Where fairy magic goes, fate follows along," Miss Dandelion says with a wave of her hand, as if this is something I should just know.

"And of course, true love breaks all unwanted spells. Normally a kiss." She cringes. "Normally. *This* is a bit of a tougher case. So, you need to go further. This requires more than true love's kiss. You need true love's intercourse."

"As in *sexual intercourse*? With a cup of bubble tea?" My eyebrows nearly fly off my scalp. Surely, I'm misunderstanding.

"Yes. And it has to be *true* love for him to transform. I'm assuming you'll need to get to know one another first to fall in love. Can you do that? Spend some time together?

The bubble tea starts laughing. Cracking up. Just absolutely losing his shit like this is the most hilarious thing to ever happen. I can't believe the nerve of this man.

"If I don't spill his ass first."

CHAPTER THREE
Adanna

"Do we really have to stop at the dog park? Fucking hell, this is emasculating." Harry, as it turns out the bubble tea man is named, says from his place strapped next to Snappy in the baby carriage.

I didn't even bother trying to put him in the drink holder, he's just too big.

"Yes. I promised Snappy we would go. Now, quit talking before someone sees you flapping your lid."

The dog park isn't far, so it doesn't take long to get there, thankfully. We enter the area that's fenced in specifically for smaller breeds. I take Snappy out and let her play. There aren't many dogs here today. The dogs here are the ones she plays with well. They don't mind if she plays off-leash with them, but of course, I'll watch out in case anyone else shows up.

Harry stays in the carriage, and I pull the shade on it down so he's not as visible if someone walks past. I figure I should try to make conversation, and it would be better if no one sees him flapping away. If someone thinks I'm talking to myself, I don't mind, but if someone sees me talking to a living bubble tea, I'll have issues.

"Alright, well, if anyone comes close, don't speak—it wouldn't be good for them to hear you and start to wonder things—but I figure we should have a chat." I smooth my pink skirt and nervously begin to fondle the lace at the edge. "I'll tell you a little about myself and then you can tell me a little about you. I already told you my name is Adanna, but that's a nickname. It's short for Adannaya. I'm a quantitative analyst. My favorite hobbies are photography and making tiny clothes for Snappy so I can post videos of her on social media. We have almost one million followers on our Tok-Talk channel, can you believe it?"

"I'd believe just about anything at this point," Harry says with a sigh.

"Ah, cheer up. I know you're a tea and everything, but at least you look like a nice flavor."

"Nice? What's your order then?" he asks.

"Milk tea. 25% sweet. Almond milk. Half the boba. Extra ice."

"Terrible." He scoffs.

"I'm prediabetic and want to avoid high sugar content. It took me a long time to perfect the order. Be nice."

"Oh. Sorry."

"Well, what about you? Tell me about yourself, Sippy."

"Okay first off, do not call me Sippy, or I'll come over there and—."

"And what? You're a cup strapped into a baby carriage."

He laughs, ice cubes clinking.

"I won't always be."

"Whatever. Big, plastic cup talking tough. You're made from compostable corn-based plastic, according to the label on your bottom. Did you know that? Better for the environment."

"I'm glad to know you noticed my bottom."

"Are you always a pervert?" I ask with a raised eyebrow.

"Only on the days when the sun rises in the east. So anyway, about me. Harry is short for Harold. Bet you never would've guessed that. I'm a writer on a television show. Thankfully, we're between seasons, so they won't miss me while I'm fixing this mess. My hobbies are baking and ice hockey. I don't have a Tok-Talk account and frankly have no idea what a quantitative analyst does."

It's my turn to laugh now, though I have no cubes to clink.

"I guess we don't have much in common since I have no interest in hockey, I don't watch much television, and my pre-diabetes keeps me from eating a lot of baked goods. Keeps me from bubble tea generally too, unless I get my special order."

There's a soft liquid swishing sound from inside the carriage.

"You know, I don't think I'm very sweet. My boba-to-milk ratio seems heavy on the milk. Something tells me you could suck up my balls."

That statement sounds obscene. I know he's telling me I could safely *drink him*, but still, I feel my cheeks heat. It feels *so naughty*.

I clear my throat as I continue to rub my fingers along the lace edge of my skirt.

"Stop that right now, you perv," I say.

"I'm sorry, ma'am. I was just admiring your top, I swear. I wasn't staring at your cleavage. It's a really lovely top," a red-haired man standing a few feet in front of me says. I hadn't noticed him before I spoke. He holds his hands up, his face red in embarrassment. His eyes dart to a woman playing with a dachshund on the other side of the park. "Don't tell my wife, okay?"

"Oh. Um. Don't do it again." I wave him off. "Leave me alone and we won't have an issue."

"Thank you. Sorry again." The man runs toward his wife without looking back.

Ice cubes clink loudly as soon as the man is gone, Harry laughing hysterically. I shake my head but can't help the smile that lifts the corners of my lips.

"Damn, that was funny," Harry says when he finally stops laughing. "That guy was scared shitless. He *was* definitely staring at your cleavage, by the way. It's impossible not to."

I adjust the ruffled collar of my shirt self-consciously.

"How can you even see? You don't have eyes."

"I don't know. Not really sure how any of this works. For example, how are we supposed to have sex? I don't have a di—"

"Okay, I get it," I cut him off quickly.

After a moment of awkward silence, he speaks again.

"I think it's probably my straw. You know. For the sex."

I sigh as his laughter begins again.

CHAPTER FOUR
Adanna

When we get back to my apartment, I heft Harry onto the kitchen table and then I feed Snappy. After that, I make myself ewa riro and fried plantains for dinner. Harry apparently doesn't feel hungry, so I don't make him anything. I don't see a way he would eat without a mouth anyway.

"This is a pretty nice place. How long have you lived here?" Harry asks. Briefly, I wonder which direction he sees from if he doesn't have eyes.

"About four years. I moved to the city for my job. It wasn't a huge move, I was born only a few cities away, but it's pretty different from where I was. I grew up in a big house in the suburbs. Uprooting everything to move into this little one-bedroom was a shock at first. When I was looking for a place, there wasn't much availability, however, so I took the first decent thing I found. Planned on getting a bigger apartment eventually but now I'm used to it. The landlord lets me decorate so that's a pretty big plus." I pat the pink kitchen wall with a smile.

"So, you're a rich girl then? Well, la-dee-da."

"My *family* is, yes. My father made his money in Nigeria working in tech before I was even born. He met my mom at a conference in the U.S. and the rest is history. They don't pay for my day-to-day life though. Once I moved out, I insisted on making my own way and I'm doing fine, even if my dad has a fit about it. He can't stand the thought of his precious daughter living alone, unprotected."

"They'll be alright having a son-in-law who isn't rich, right? I mean, I'm not broke, don't get me wrong. It's just that television writers aren't rolling in dough. Unfortunately, I love the work regardless of the pay."

"I think you should be more concerned about whether or not *I'd* accept you as a husband. You just dropped that son-in-law thing in there like it's a given. Weird behavior, Harry." I give him the side-eye as I pick him up and carry him to the living room.

"Well, we're supposed to be falling in love and all of that. I write shows about true love. I know how it goes. Besides, I'm a romantic. Once we fall in love, I want a wedding and a honeymoon and a happily-ever-after." His ice and boba jiggle around merrily when I set him on the coffee table.

I plop onto the sofa in front of him, relaxing into the cushions. Snappy's wet nose tickles my ankle as she urges me to pick her up. Bending to lift her feels like an incredible chore. I'm exhausted. A yawn escapes my lips as I stroke the dog's soft fur.

"Sounds like you could use some sleep," says Harry.

"You're not wrong." I stretch my neck from side to side, enjoying the cracks and pops.

Ice cubes tinkle from atop my coffee table.

"Yeah, that's the good stuff," Harry chuckles. "No stretching here though. Not much of anything here."

I stand up and bend backward enough to let my spine do a little popping too.

"Don't worry. We'll have you moving one way or another."

Chapter Five
Adanna

"So, do you feel anything? What's it like?"

I washed up early for the day, put on my nightgown and bonnet, and lay down on the bed, Harry on my bedside table.

"It's weird. I instinctually knew how to do some stuff right away, like talk, and look around, but I can't figure out other stuff, like how we're expected to have magical sex or whatever. However, I still think it's gotta be the straw. Oh, I discovered this while you were in the shower." Harry pauses for a few seconds before there's a sudden squeaking sound as his straw slides in and out of his opening quickly.

"Oh, eew stop that!" I wave my hands in front of me. "That cannot be it. Please no."

"I'm just saying it could be related to something. I don't exactly have many other skills."

"Yes, I know, but it's incredibly unsexy. Those rigid plastic edges scraping my insides sounds like torture."

I lay on my side and watch the boba shift around his milky insides like a dull lava lamp. *What exactly are we supposed to do? Well, there's the obvious.*

"Maybe I'm supposed to drink you. Why else would you be my favorite order if I wasn't supposed to?"

The boba shifts rapidly in his milk tea, ice clinking loudly.

"I—I think I like that idea, Adanna. Just, uh, be gentle. No one likes a straw biter."

I smooth my hands down over my loose cotton garment.

"Hmm. I'm not exactly feeling sexy. I've got a granny-style nightdress on, and somehow, I'm supposed to seduce you so well that you fall desperately in love with me?"

"Those nightgowns worked just fine for plenty of grannies. My grandma had eight kids, was married sixty years, and only wore cotton nightgowns. Must be something to them."

I shake my head as I laugh. "I think that was more than likely social pressure and lack of birth control but sure, we can go with the nightdress."

"So, how's about it? A little sippy-sip?" His straw makes that annoying squeak again.

I prop my head on my hand and squint at him.

"Are you this frustrating as a man?"

"As a man, I have far more ways to be annoying than I do as a cup of tea. This is nothing. But don't worry, I promise to use them all to be adorable."

Sighing, I sit up and swing my legs over the edge of the bed.

"You are annoying as hell. I'll take a sip, but I'm telling you right now, I do not want to have to put this straw between my downstairs lips. That is not a way I can personally see myself expressing love."

"Oh, come on now. True love takes all forms of expression. Have you read James Joyce's love letters to Nora Barnacle? I was reading them the other day. They were deeply in love, and he talks an awful lot about how he loves her fa—"

I hold my hand up.

"Yes, I have read them. And if you want any chance of romance tonight you will stop talking about them. That is a mood killer like nothing else."

His ice cubes clink as he chuckles.

"Alright, alright."

"Now, no squeaking straw. And keep your lid closed."

"Yes, ma'am."

My cheeks feel warm all of a sudden and my palms start to sweat. *Why am I feeling so nervous? It's just a little sip.* I gently hold the base of his straw with my first two fingers and my thumb, lean forward, and slide the end between my puckered lips. He's such a big drink that he requires a thicker-than-normal straw, which means I have to suck harder than I would with a regular-sized beverage. As the liquid starts to rise in the straw a soft groan comes from under Harry's lid.

I nearly pause at the sound, my whole body flushing with heat. My nipples harden, brushing the fabric of my nightdress. A light whimper escapes me as I suck harder.

Finally, the liquid splashes against my tongue. It tastes divine. My perfect order. Milky, slightly sweet, with a tiny hint of bitterness. I keep sucking. It's so *good*. I picture the man on the bench moaning under me instead of this cup, dark hair falling over his brow, cheeks flushed, lips popping open, his gazing locking onto mine.

"Oh fuck. Keep going. Get the boba. Fuck yes," Harry pants from out of his lid.

His speech breaks my spell. *This is a motherfucking cup of tea.*

I pull back and shake my head. Doing it for the spell is one thing but actually getting turned on by it is another. That's fucked up. I look back to Harry to try to explain. My eyes grow wide. *Oh hell no.*

"What the fuck is that?" I shout.

"Uh, you know, I think *that* might be my dick," Harry says as the *bulge* on top of him slowly shrinks. "At least the start of it anyway. It's going away now."

"I just don't understand what the hell was happening there. Why did it look like—" I flail my arms in confusion, "like *that*?"

"Like I *said*," he sasses back, "I don't think it was fully grown yet. As to why it was clear like that, I think it's because that's just the color of my...skin. If the cup is considered my skin, that is."

My face wrinkles in disgust. I suppose the cup is kind of like his skin, but I don't want to *think* about that. As for the thing that was growing on him, it was indeed clear like his cup, and started growing up out of his lid. It went straight up along with the direction of his straw, but much, much thicker than it. It wasn't smooth like his straw though; it was textured all along the whole thing. It only made it about halfway up the height of the straw before I pulled away, but if it had gone all the way up, I could imagine it would have looked something like, I don't know, a mostly transparent corncob with a straw running up the center.

A thought hits me.

"Oh, I can't believe it. You're dick's not the straw—it's corn. You have a crystal-clear corncob cock."

I fall backward onto the mattress and laugh so hard my stomach hurts. It takes a couple of minutes for me to finish laughing, but when I finally do I sit back up and wipe the tears from my eyes. If a cup could look annoyed, Harry would.

"You done?" he grumps.

"For now."

"It's because of the corn-based plastic then, I'm guessing?"

"I'm guessing so. Could be worse. There are a lot of potentially nightmarish alternatives should it have been made from the milk."

"Corn is definitely the better option, yes. So, uh, now that we know what it is, does that mean you're interested in continuing what we were doing earlier? Because I'm fully prepared to pop this corn."

I close my eyes and sigh.

"You're nasty. But that's not why I'm saying no for the evening. All this drama has just put me out of the mood. Get some sleep."

I scoot back into bed and tuck myself under the covers, reach over to the side table, and switch off the lamp.

"Didn't sound like you thought I was nasty when you were drinking me earlier."

"Goodnight, Harry."

CHAPTER SIX

Harry

"**H**ot damn, you look good!" I exclaim from the top of the dresser as Adanna gives me a twirl, showing off her outfit of the day.

It's time for her to do her daily video for that Tok-Talk thing. Snappy and her apparently do a video every morning that's a mix of style and financial education. I might be a living bubble tea that desperately needs her help, but she has greater priorities.

"Thank you, Harry." She gently boops me on the edge of my lid. "Come on, Snappy!"

The little dog comes running into the room, pink tongue poking out. Adanna scoops her up and spins around before setting Snappy onto her get-ready bench.

Yes, the dog has its own area in the room with its furniture. I guess it normally sleeps in there too but last night was an exception. She was afraid Snappy might spill me. Wonder if the dog will still sleep in there after Adanna and I get married.

Adanna seems to think it's odd that I'm so confident about us having a happily-ever-after once I'm out of beverage form. I don't see why I shouldn't be sure about it. Seems obvious to me. If she's the one who turns me back into a man then that's just fairytale rules, right? Besides, she's hot, smart, and I like listening to her talk. If there's one thing you should look for in a partner, it's someone you like listening to.

"Okay, my little puppy, let's get ready to tell the people all about today's finance tips!" Adanna says as she picks up the doggy brush and goes to work carefully separating Snappy's fur into sections for bows.

"Maybe someday I can brush your hair. Ever since I first saw you, I've thought it

was so—" I start to say before Adanna raises a hand, palm out, to silence me.

"If you mess with my hair, I'll kill you."

"What? What if I promise to be gentle?"

"I don't play about my hair, Sippy. It
takes too much time and money to keep it
the way I like it for you to go putting your
grubby fingers in it." She stops brushing
Snappy for a moment to point the brush at
me. "Keep away."

"Is that why you wear a hat to bed? To
protect your hair?"

"A *hat*? It's called a bonnet." She shakes
her head and mumbles under her breath,
"What is my mother going to think of this
man?"

"Don't worry, moms love me. The show
I write for performs well in that demo-
graphic."

"And what show is that? You never told
me."

"It's called Cherry Ridge Hospital."

It's a hospital drama with a lot of
steamy romance and angst to keep people
tuned in every week.

"I've heard of it. And yes, my mom does watch it. I wouldn't have thought of you as the romantic drama series type." She raises an eyebrow at me.

"There's a lot you don't know about me. I think you'll be pleasantly surprised at what you find." My ice cubes clink like they do when I'm feeling particularly happy.

They sure do clink a lot when Adanna's in the room.

Snappy sits perfectly still while my darling gets her ready for the day in a collar to match her outfit. Soon, she's ready, and the two film the short video. I don't understand a lick of what Adanna says—it's all portfolios this and equity that—but I enjoy watching her, nonetheless.

"All done," she says as she taps to upload, "Now, how's my favorite beverage man?"

"Favorite? I'll have you know I killed Dr. Pepper in his sleep, so you'll have to settle for me."

She huffs out a short laugh. Got it. I love her laugh. Her long fingers with their painted-pink nails pat the clouds of curls atop her head as she rolls her eyes at me and clicks her tongue.

"What am I going to do with you?"

"Hopefully something sexy," I say, my ice cubes jiggling a little as I try to hold back a laugh.

"Okay, that's enough out of you," she picks me up and offers me a wry look.

I can't help but antagonize her just a little.

"Really sexy. Smutty even."

"You get on my nerves." She carries me out into the kitchen and sets me on the counter.

"Like dirty enough that I couldn't even work it into a script for cable. Here, let me give you some ideas. First—"

"I'm gonna dump you down the sink." Adanna takes a big bite out of a banana.

My ice cubes clink together loudly as I cackle with mirth. I just can't help it.

"Ah, you're beautiful, Adanna. Truly."

She rolls her big, brown eyes again but this time it feels more like she's doing it to avoid looking at me. *Shy all of a sudden, is she?* A moment later she's rinsing off her hands and gathering up Snappy to secure the both of us for the morning walk.

"What's stochastic calculus? I heard you mention it when filming your video and I've never heard that term before," I ask as we head out the door.

"Asking me to talk nerdy? Now you're really trying to flirt. Hmm. Alright, where to start? What do you know about Brownian motion?"

I was indeed trying to flirt but I also do want to know more about what she does and who she is. So, I ask question after question as we walk—well, when no one else is around to hear me, anyway. The whole being a drink thing does get in the way of public conversation.

"And that's the best way I can explain the Monte Carlo Simulation. Does that make sense?" she asks.

She's tried to explain this to me for the last half hour and I still have no idea what the simulation is even supposed to accomplish. I am not made out for STEM. My mind is a liberal arts zone. All I asked was why it was called the Monte Carlo Simulation when she referred to it in a different confusing discussion. Honestly, I don't think she ever even gave me the answer to that. Doesn't matter, I could still listen to her talk all day.

"Makes total sense. When do you have to go back to work, by the way? The math mines don't dig themselves, I assume."

"Monday, unfortunately. I'm worried about it too. I don't want to leave you home alone, but I can't bring you to work with me."

You could just fall in love with me and get freaky. Easy solution. I change the topic.

"Speaking of home, if you don't have anything else to do today, we could go visit my house. Make sure no one broke in and killed my plants. It's not far from the park."

"How will we get in though? I didn't suggest we go to your place because I assumed we wouldn't be able to get into an apartment without keys. Whatever keys you had are now part of your whole deal."

"I live in a house, not an apartment. And I hide an extra key outside, under a fake plant." My milk tea sloshes slightly when a feeling of disgust comes over me. "Everything is all just up in here with me, huh? Everything I had in my pockets. My shoes. Phone. All of it."

The amount of germs and stuff that must be mixed up with me right now? Yuck.

Adanna appears in front of the carriage with Snappy in her arms and a disapproving look on her face.

"You leave your keys under a plant? That's dumb as hell, Harry. Anyone could find that key and break in. *Tsk.*"

"What can I say, I'm a fool," I say as Adanna clips Snappy in next to me. I jiggle my wet and sloppies around inside my cup. "A fool for love."

"Just give me the directions to your house."

We enjoy the lovely May weather on the short walk to my house. There are people around, so we don't get to talk much, but that's alright—just being near her is a treasure. When we arrive at the destination, she picks up the plant I told her to and sighs at me when she finds the key there. She might disapprove of my methods, but she has to admit they worked out in my favor this time.

Unfortunately, I don't have a ramp, and hauling my liquidy behind up the stairs in the stroller would be a struggle. She decides to leave the stroller outside. Adanna, Snappy, and I enter my little blue house together.

"Sorry, it's not very exciting. Hope you didn't expect a big reveal," I say.

"I'm glad it's not shocking, honestly. I don't think I could use another surprise." She picks a book up off of my coffee table. "Simone de Beauvoir, huh?"

I feel pretty confident that she thinks I'm a cool, intellectual type for about two seconds before she picks up the next book.

"Twilig—"

"It was research, okay?" I cut her off.

"Whatever floats your boat." She sets the book back down and we continue to tour my little house.

It isn't very exciting, I wasn't lying. The decor is fairly sparse, the place is clean. It doesn't scream "heavily lived in." After she lugs me into my bedroom and notices my sparse wardrobe, she finally comments on it.

"Alright, are you a minimalist or something?"

"Nah. Just don't spend a lot of time here. I spend most of my time working with the other writers. It's a pretty popular show with twenty-two episodes a season so we're kept busy. When I'm not writing for a series, I'm writing something else, focused on the screen. My main hobby is hockey, so that's outside of the house with my friends. I usually fly home to my family when we're on hiatus rather than bum around town, just happened not to this time. I don't know, that just means I don't need *stuff*."

She sits on my queen-sized bed with its navy blue comforter and white sheets and sets me on my oak side table.

"I suppose that makes sense, but I like *stuff* so if we're going to be together you better get used to having unnecessary knickknacks around. Sometimes I like having things just to come home to something pretty."

"Well, I'd already have *you* so I wouldn't need anything else pretty, but I get your point. I'd like to address the fact that you're speaking of our future together. I'm glad you've come to terms with it."

"Hey now, I said *if* we're going to be together. That's no guarantee. I'll try to help you, of course, but I'm not promising you I'll fall in love with you."

She crosses her arms in front of her self-consciously and looks away from me. I know she's not in love with me yet. That's fine. But she will be. It's fate. I'll just give fate a boost.

CHAPTER SEVEN
Harry

We head out, stop to grab some food to go for Adanna, and then return to her apartment. She and Snappy eat and afterward Snappy curls up for a nap. It's just my darling and me alone in the quiet.

"You said earlier you visit your family. Are they far?" she asks.

We're sitting in the living room, her on the sofa and me on the end table. She's absentmindedly running her finger up and down my side, wiping streaks through my condensation. It's making me nervous. I don't feel much physically on my cup, but the *idea* of it has my straw aching. I worry I'm going to pop my cob if she keeps it up.

"Uh, yeah. They're in Alberta. Canada."

"Canadian? That explains the hockey thing then," she smiles.

"Hey now, that's a stereotype. Plenty of places like hockey. It's an Olympic sport."

"Don't get grumpy, I'm just messing with you."

"I'm not grumpy, I'm just saying—"

The finger she's been sliding up and down my cup continues up past my lid and onto my straw. Adanna carefully pinches the base between her thumb and first two fingers. A millimeter at most, she raises my straw and then pushes it back down. Out, then in. This in-and-out jerk-off coming out of nowhere scrambles my brain entirely.

"Just saying what, Harry?" she purrs.

"Some, uh, nothing," I sputter back.

"There we go."

It takes me a second to figure out what she's referring to but when she stops jerking my straw off and starts stroking toward the top of it instead, I see what she means. My biodegradable, renewable resource is making an appearance. Hello once again, my corn-based plastic friend.

"I'm gonna take you to my bedroom now, alright?" she asks as she lifts me, knowing full well I'll say yes.

"Fine with me."

When we get to her room, she sets me to the side before laying a blanket on the open area of the floor and then setting me on the center of the blanket.

"I can't put you on the bed. Don't want you to spill." She shrugs.

I laugh.

"I appreciate your concern. I like the view from down here anyway."

And a nice view it is. Right up her little skirt.

"I suppose I can't tell you off for being a pervert now since we're about to—yeah." She looks away as she gets on her knees on the floor.

"We're about to fuck, you mean," I state matter of factly.

"You don't have to say it like that!" She shoots me an annoyed look. "But yeah, that."

"Adanna, it's okay. Don't be shy about it. You weren't shy in the living room just now."

"That's different. We were talking and it just happened. It wasn't focused on—I don't know. This is so weird."

"It is weird. But I am head over heels in love with you already Adanna. From the moment I saw you I knew magic was in the air. What else could it be? The way the sunlight glittered like diamonds on your brown skin, and you had that fluffy pink cupcake of a skirt, the halo of curls—you couldn't be anything but a fairy-tale princess." I pause when she lays her hand against my side, but when she goes no further, I continue. "I'm still a man, under all this. It seems silly because of the form I'm in but make no mistake—it's a real heart you hold in your hands. Please don't break it."

A breath shudders out of her. She nods her head once.

"Alright. Let's do this." She takes hold of the edge of her shirt and lifts it over her head.

Fuck yes.

"Might as well get comfy," she says with a short laugh.

"Get as comfortable as you want."

She unclasps her bra, her breasts falling free. My clear cock begins growing anew at the sight of her hard, dark nipples. *Fuck I can't wait until I have a mouth again.* Adanna shimmies out of her skirt, and she's left in nothing but tiny, pink panties. She sits in front of me, legs spread teasingly, casually running her hand along her thigh.

"Adanna, I swear to god if you don't take off those panties right now—"

"You'll what?"

I'll do nothing. Damn it.

"Silence. That's what I thought." She laughs. "Don't worry, I was just looking at you, I wasn't trying to tease you too long."

"Looking?" I try to inspect myself but obviously can't see everything. "What's the verdict?"

"Nice and thick. Textured. I can see through it to where the straw runs up the center."

I chuckle at the image in my mind, but the sound is cut off when she grips my cock in her soft fist.

"Mm. Firm, but squishy. Not rigid like plastic thankfully." She runs her fist up and down several times, making me groan, before she stops at the top. She places her thumb over what was the opening of my straw but feels different now. "Your straw opening is under this slit here. I'm assuming you'll come out of the straw, and then out of here."

"Let's find out, shall we?" I choke out.

"Let's go, then."

Adanna stands, takes hold of the sides of her panties, then drags them down her long legs. She positions herself over me, holding onto the bed for balance.

Yeah, the view down here is pretty nice.

Her hand wraps around me once again, guiding me toward her glistening entrance. *It's finally happening.* She sighs as she drags the head of my cock along her wet seam. I'm speechless. Until she aligns me with her center and slowly begins to sink, that is.

"Oh, fuck," I moan, "Feels so good. Don't stop."

"I don't intend to," she strains out as she forces herself lower.

"Are you okay?"

"Yes, just been a while. Feels good though."

"Good. I want you to like it. Like me. Oh, fuck." My mind goes blank when her bottom hits my lid. We fit perfectly together.

"There we go," she pants out, "you fit me just right, Harry."

"We're made for each—" I'm cut off in garbled syllables when Adanna starts working her hips, riding me rhythmically.

"Your texture feels amazing. Oh god, Harry, your cock is fantastic."

She rides me faster, holding onto the bed for stability, which I appreciate, as I do not want an accidental slip knocking me sideways. Her internal walls drag along the textured surface of my compostable cock, creating a sensation unlike anything I've ever felt before. It's absolutely magical.

"Touch yourself, Adanna. Come for me," I rasp. If I had hands, I'd reach around and do it myself, but I was only given so many extra parts today.

"Yes, yes," she says as she rubs her clit in fast circles. The wet sound drives me mad, and I can feel something besides tea brewing inside me.

"Adanna, I think I can feel it," I strain to say.

"Me too," she whines, right before her cunt clamps around me. "Oh, fuck. Harry!"

Wetness runs down her inner thighs and onto my lid. *Fuck yes.* My lid is drenched in her pleasure. It's the final key to unlocking my own orgasm.

"I'm gonna spill, Adanna," I groan as I feel heaviness rise up my straw, "right into your pretty pussy."

And then it happens—my boba erupts from my straw, forcing the slit in my corncob cock wide open. I let out a long, low moan as the tapioca pearls spill into her passage, packing themselves tightly inside her, filling every crevice. When I'm done, I notice Adanna is still and silent.

"Mm, that was good, wasn't it?" I sigh, hoping she agrees. I mean, she has to agree...right?

"Uh, yeah. Until the boba. What the fuck?"

It really does not sound like she agrees.

"What's wrong with the boba?" I ask, confused.

"What do you mean what's wrong? There's a ton of tapioca inside me. I'm afraid to even move. How am I supposed to get it all out? You should have warned me!" She snaps.

"I assumed you'd expect it. It seemed obvious to me. I'm a bubble tea! When you thought of sex with a bubble tea what else did you think would come out?"

"I don't know, tea? Maybe a couple of boba. Not *all* of them! How are they all packed up there? Son of a—I'm going to go try to take care of this I guess."

"Please don't be upset. Adanna?"

She drags herself off of me—I manage to stifle the hiss of lingering pleasure as she does—and heads toward the bathroom. Several boba tumble out of her as she goes. Mumbled curse words follow her.

Damn. This isn't how I wanted it to go. I expected her to fall in love with me and then I'd magically turn into a man. We'd—

My ice cubes shake. *Odd.*

Oh, Adanna. Please come back soon. I promise things will be better. I—

The plastic on my sides begins to stretch out and back in again. My lid wobbles around and around. *Okay, something's happening.* My whole cup grows taller by a foot.

Poof I'm a man again, sitting on the bed, just as I was on the bench at the park. Even still have my drink in my hand.

I slam the bubble tea down onto Adanna's side table—I don't think I ever want to see one of those again. With a quickness,

I run to the bathroom and knock on the door.

"Adanna!" I shout, "It worked!"

The door flies open a few seconds later. She has a towel wrapped around herself, her eyes are wide, and her jaw dropped.

"Oh my god! Harry? Is it really you?"

"Yes! It's really me! No more flapping lid!" I laugh.

"Harry! We did it!" Adanna jumps, wrapping her arms and legs around me.

Our first kiss is divine. The real joy between us is tangible. I take in every gasp of pleasure she offers and save it. I'll save every one she ever gives me and one day when she needs extra love, I'll return the pleasure tenfold. She's going to be mine forever and I need to take care of her.

She pulls away and I carry her to the bedroom.

"We did do it. Well, you did. I mostly just sat there, thinking about how wonderful you are."

I lay her on the bed then lay down beside her. Finally being able to stroke the soft skin of her cheek with my hand is a gift I'll never take for granted.

"You're a sweet talker," she laughs.

"Only twenty-five percent sweet. I'm being tame because of the whole prediabetes thing."

"Terrible. Absolutely terrible joke."

"Well, what can I say, I normally have an entire room of writers to help me with jokes. I'm more of the romantic storyline guy."

She looks at me with a smile that turns heated quickly. Her eyes drag up and down my body lustfully once before returning to my stomach and staying locked there, confused.

"What?" I ask, sitting up to get a better look at myself.

She raises my shirt and then pushes down the waistband of my pants. I see then what the issue is.

I'm still see-through on my lower half.

CHAPTER EIGHT
Harry

We return to the park bench where I got turned into a bubble tea, hoping to figure out what the hell is going on. We did what we were supposed to do so why am I all messed up?

"Miss Dandelion? Mrs. Petunia?" Adanna asks for the fourth time. "Please, if you're here can you help us?"

Finally, we both sit on the bench, hunched over in defeat. How are we supposed to fix this? Half of my body is plastic and filled with tea. I even have the corncob dick with a straw and everything. This time though the straw goes into my balls where little boba are. It's fucking weird. Adanna won't have sex with me. It sucks.

"I guess we give up then?" I say.

"Give up? On what?" A small voice says from beside me.

On the side opposite Adanna stands Miss Dandelion. She looks frazzled, her hair half falling out of her bun.

"Oh, thank goodness, you're here," Adanna says. "We need your help."

"Everyone needs my help today. May is a busy month for a fairy." Miss Dandelion plops down on the bench beside me, her tiny legs barely dangling off the edge. "What can I do for you?"

"Well, we did the, uh, necessary activity and I turned back into a man, as you can see," I say gesturing to myself.

Miss Dandelion nods approvingly.

"But he's still tea on his bottom half," Adanna finishes.

"Hmm." Miss Dandelion concentrates, tapping her chin and shaking her leg as she focuses. After a moment she sits up straight and snaps. "Oh, it's obvious. One of you still has reservations about the happily ever after love part. Once that's settled, you'll be fine."

Miss Dandelion pats my leg and stands up.

"So, both of us just need to be in true love, and then my body will be fixed?" I swallow nervously as my eyes dart to a sheepish-looking Adanna.

"That's right. The closer you get to love, the closer you get to human again." Miss Dandelion stretches her arms and yawns. "If that's all, I've got a whole bunch of angry ladybugs with no spots to get back to."

"That's it. Thank you," Adanna says.

With a *poof* Miss Dandelion is gone.

An awkward silence hangs between us as we walk back to Adanna's apartment. The impending discussion follows behind, whistling a funeral march.

When we arrive, she feeds Snappy and then we both sit across from each other at the kitchen table. I tap my fingers nervously waiting to see if she speaks first but she's occupied with stroking the lace edge of her skirt and staring at the floor. So, I clear my throat.

"I'm all in, Adanna. You know that by now. I'm planning to be with you forever and I'm beyond happy with that. So, we both know you're the unsure one."

After a beat, Adanna nods without looking up.

"I feel guilty. It's my fault your body is like that," she says quietly.

"It's not your fault. It's some fairy's fault. You didn't accidentally curse me. You have no reason to feel guilty. I need you to understand that. This is not your fault. Even if I had remained a cup of tea forever because you wanted nothing to do with me and just left me on that bench it wouldn't have been your fault. It's the fault of the fairy who turned me. Not you."

"Yeah, but—"

"Adanna," I lean over the table and put my hand on her cheek. She looks up into my eyes. "It is not your fault. Okay?"

"Okay." She exhales heavily.

Reluctantly I release her and sit back in my seat.

"I understand that you might not believe in happily ever after yet. You're a crazy smart person. Logically none of this makes sense. Meeting someone and fully believing *they're the one* within a few days is crazy. So, take your time. If it takes you weeks, months, or years, I'll still be here. Like I said, I'm all in. I'm not going anywhere. I'll be here when you're ready. I'll just have a crystal-clear corncob cock while I'm waiting."

And wait I did.

We dated for weeks. I got to see her in her business wear. Wool pants, plain blouses, with her hair pulled back into a bun? Carrying a laptop and a giant thermos of coffee? Was like seeing a totally different person. As soon as work ended, however, she'd come home and return to her bubbly self. I've still been on hiatus and feeling like the world's biggest bum. At least she hasn't had to pay for doggy daycare since I can watch Snappy. I return to work soon though.

Tonight I took her to a hockey game. We met some of my friends and they got along really well. Adanna said the hockey "outfits" were sexy and she wants to see me in mine sometime. I have never been so ready to put on a jersey in my life. Once the game was over and we said bye to my friends, we drove back to her house.

I've been sleeping over every night. We've taken things a lot slower than we did when I was tea. There's been a lot of kissing and touching but nothing more than that. I'm moving at her pace. It's going well though. I know it is because I'm becoming steadily more solid. One of my legs is completely solid again. Not a trace of plastic in it. The other foot is fully normal too. She's falling for me, just like I knew she would.

"Hey there," I say with a smile, so close my lips brush against hers. We're lying facing each other in bed, only the faint trace of moonlight from the tiny crack between the curtains lighting the room.

"Hey to you too." She sets her palm against my chest, right against my heart. I close my eyes and enjoy the feeling of her so close to my life source. *I'd give it to you if you asked.* "I had fun tonight. Your friends were great."

"They liked you a lot. I hope your friends like me when I finally get to meet them." A little hint, as I have not yet been invited to anything.

"Well, I do have a wedding to go to in a few weeks. But you can't go wearing anything from that sad wardrobe you have. You have to look ten out of ten at Nigerian celebrations." She props herself up on her elbow. "And please tell me you can dance even a little bit."

"Hey, I've got moves!"

"You've got moves, huh?" She nips my bottom lip. "You wanna show me some moves?"

Hot damn.

"Yeah?" I bite her lip back, just a little bit harder. "Well, then. May I have this dance?"

She chuckles softly. "You are so corny."

"A little bit still, yeah." I kiss the end of her adorably round nose, then shift my body so that she's underneath me.

"That's not what I meant," she says, pushing up at my chest.

I snatch her hand and drag it above her head. I take the second and hold it there as well. She sighs when I kiss her neck, softly at first, growing harder and faster as I get closer to her chest.

"Oh, Harry. I want you to take me tonight. I don't care about your...situation. I need to feel you inside me." Every word is a plea and a confession. "Now."

Oh, thank God, it's teatime.

CHAPTER NINE
Adanna

Alright, he's still got a bubble tea dick. Things could be a lot worse. He could still be a cup. That would be *much* worse. I wouldn't be feeling any of what I am right now if that were the case.

"Fuck, Adanna, you taste so good." Harry's voice is muffled between my thighs.

I run my fingers through his soft, silky hair. His tongue is rough against my clit, his fingers curving in and out of me at a steady pace. His other hand grabs hold of one of mine and he threads our fingers together. The licking pressure of his tongue shifts to a more insistent pressure. I squeeze his hand as my hips rise off the mattress.

"Yes, yes, Harry!" I shout as I come in the dark, my thighs tightly pressing against him.

After a moment, he pushes himself up to my height, panting. I can see his comfortable smile made cocky by this victory. Obviously, I can't help but to kiss the guy.

"That was so good," I say when we pull away from the kiss.

"Yes you were," Harry says before planting kisses down my neck.

"When are you going to take these off, Sippy?" I tug at the waistband of his black boxer briefs. He's been resisting every time I try to take them off tonight so far and I don't think he realizes I've noticed.

"Are you going to keep calling me Sippy?"

"Sometimes. Now answer my question."

"I just don't want to ruin the night by scaring you off." He runs a hand down the side of my face. "I'm fine with doing things just for you."

"Hey, you stop that. As you've told me many times, I'm hot, smart, and rich. I'm laying here bare ass naked begging you to fuck me. You're really gonna say no?" I raise an eyebrow and watch his soft expression crack into a wide grin. "Yeah, I didn't think so."

Shortly after, he's bottomless. One good thing is his second leg is now fully solid. Bad thing—well, I'm not gonna worry about that. It'll still do the job.

I pull Harry's face to mine and kiss him deeply as he lines his cock up with my entrance. He's a fantastic kisser. Every kiss, no matter if it's a brief kiss goodbye or a passionate kiss in bed, feels important. It seems to me as if I'm something truly precious to him. That he really, really does *love* me.

And, damn it, I do love him.

Harry groans as his cock breaches my opening, its textured surface dragging slowly up my wet walls. I'd forgotten how good that feels. I'll miss it when it's gone.

Because it will be gone. I know now that I truly love him.

Maybe I can convince him to buy a textured toy for us to play with someday. The thought makes a giggle bubble out of me.

"What's so funny?" he pants out.

"Nothing. Don't stop." I wrap my legs around him. "Don't stop."

I have to admit, he does have moves. No lies were told. He may be a little on the skinny side but he's strong. Has no problem tossing me in any position. As he's got me on all fours, ass to the heavens, I can't help but think *why did I wait all those weeks? I could have been doing this all along.*

"Fuck, your ass is hot," he squeezes my hips and drives hard into me. "Your pussy feels so good. So fucking good. You gotta come for me, Adanna. Show me how you feel."

Harry pulls me against his chest, holding me against him with one arm, and uses his other hand to rub circles against my clit. I cry out in pleasure as he fucks up into me, dragging his teeth against my neck, and continues to stimulate my clit. It doesn't take long before I come hard around him. Harry comes right after I do, and the moan he lets out is hot enough to keep me coming strong.

When we're both drained, we lay back, hearts still racing, arms around each other. I nuzzle my face into his chest to hide my goofy grin. When I look upwards, I see that he's not trying to hide his at all.

"That was fun," he says, smile about a mile wide. "We should do it again some-time."

"Yeah, maybe," I say with a laugh.

"It's convenient that you finally fell truly in love with me *before* the finish. No boba."

"Wait—what?" I sit up and, sure enough, no boba. Just the regular sticky mess one would expect from this sort of encounter.

"See? I knew we were meant to be."

"You're annoying." I shove a pillow between his face and mine.

"But you love it." He pulls the pillow out of the way and kisses me on the end of my nose. "And I love you."

"Maybe you were better as a cup." I snatch the pillow back.

"Nah. Then I couldn't run you a bubble bath and make you a late-night snack."

"Is that what you're planning on doing?"

"Yep. Now you just need to decide on what you want for a snack. I know you like fruit at night. I could cut up strawberries. I know you don't like when the green top is on them."

I toss the pillow to the side and smile widely. He's such a sweetheart.

"That sounds great. But how about you make me a drink too. I could go for, I don't know—"

"Don't say it," he groans.

"—a bubble tea."

"You're lucky you're so beautiful, you know that?" He gives me the side-eye as he puts his underwear on.

"I am, I know."

He stands up and starts to head to the door.

"I'll get that bubble bath going." He pauses, then turns to me. "Oh, I forgot to ask. When you were doing your video this morning you mentioned something in your calculus talk called the Wiener Process. That can't be real, right?"

I can't help but laugh. We're going to have such a sweet life.

THE SENTIENT OBJECT HOLIDAY SERIES

The Sentient Object Holiday Series Celebrates the Following Holidays With These Books:

- *International Rubber Ducky Day,* January 13th

- *My Date With a Rubber Duckie* by Thea Masen

- *International Sweatpants Day,* January 21st

- *My Date With a Pair of Sweatpants* by Dakota Cockaday

- *National White T-shirt Day,* February 11th

- *My Date With a White T-shirt* by Dakota Cockaday

- *World Water Day, March 22nd*

- *My Date With Water* by Unfortunate Reads

- *Edible Book Day, April 1st*

- *My Date With an Edible Book* by Holly Wilde

- *International Tea Day, May 21st*

- *My Date With Bubble Tea* by Sylvia Morrow

- *International Caps Lock Day, June 28th*

- *My Date With Caps Lock* by Thea Masen

- *World UFO Day, July 2nd*

- *My Date With an Unidentified Flying Object* by Luna Cantrip

- *World Rock, Paper, Scissors Day,* August 27th

- *My Date With Rock, Paper, & Scissors* by Holly Wilde

- *World Ampersand Day,* September 8th

- *My Date With an Ampersand* by Nicole Parker

- *National LED Light Day,* October 7th

- *My Date With a Light Bulb* by Vera Valentine

- *Leif Erikson Day,* October 9th

- *My Date With a Leif Erikson Statue* by Biblio Barbie

- *World Jellyfish Day,* November 3rd

- *My Date With a Jellyfish* by Unfortunate Reads

- *International Mountain Day, December 11th*

- *My Date With a Mountain* by Luna Cantrip

You Can Find All the Books on Amazon!

SPECIAL NOTE TO READERS

Please thank Dakota Cockaday's sweat-
pants for the brief mention of James
Joyce's farty love letters, and thank Nicole
Parker for the Wiener (Process.)

About the Authors

Sylvia Morrow

Sylvia is two confused corgis in a leopard print jacket. She writes books that have been called "so weird, but so hot." You can find her Amazon author profile, social media, and links to other important information on her website at https://sylviamorrow.carrd.co/

Biblio Barbie

Biblio Barbie, Diva of Dong or...
Danelle

A lover of all things monster, sentient, paranormal and alien. She started a bookstagram in July of 2023 and quickly found a love for books all over again. Her book besties convinced her to try this indie author thing out and she started writing her first book in July of 2024 after a dumb insta poll where said friends encouraged her to write a mascot romance story. She is probably most known for her unique and excessive collection of monster *ahem* parts. She lives in the beautiful state of Colorado but doesn't consider herself an "outdoorsy kind of girl". Eyeroll. Danelle has a human husband (sigh, kidding), a son and two dogs. Danelle loves monsters of all kinds but especially wolfy men, orcs and minotaurs. She has yet to read a sentient object she didn't enjoy. Ok, there was that one… You can find her on Instagram (@biblio.ba rbie) talking about monster parts, unique rating meters, Shrek and probably hot dogs. Idk she's weird.

Dakota Cockaday
Dakota Cockaday is the pen name of the most unexciting woman in the world. Dakota loves paranormal and true crime podcasts, romance books about aliens, and chicken tamales. She always wants to pet

your dog or see pictures of your cat. Dakota hoards blank notebooks like it's her job. She has no spare time, so she writes when she really should be cleaning the house. You can reach her at dakota.cockaday@gmail.com.

Holly Wilde

Holly Wilde is the author of many ridiculously cringeable, yet deliciously bingeable, sentient object romances.

Sentient-smutty-smut and literal personification of everyday items is what you'll find in her books. Enjoy the ride and remember, if you don't buckle your seatbelt, your chair might just do it for you.

Luna Cantrip

Luna is just another weirdo turning her love of cryptozoology into smut. She writes about big soft cinnamon-roll monsters falling into gross gushy love. Her biggest dream in life is for everyone to find the perfect hairy beast who will make us

tea, read us a good book, and rip our ene-
mies in half if we ask them to very nicely.
When she's got writer's block she likes to
bake bread. She lives in Kentucky with her
husband, a cat, and another cat.
If you like anything here try and follow
her on TikTok or Instagram, because her
personality is probably better in smaller
portions anyway.

Nicole Parker

Nicole Parker is an AuDHD 30-something
California native who spends the great ma-
jority of her free time writing books, reading books, or organizing her ever-growing
TBR list. She also has a spouse, some kids,
and pets, but this isn't about them. Nicole's
books are funny, raunchy, silly, and most
importantly, full of good vibes and happy
endings.
She got into publishing in 2024 after quickly falling in love with the sentient object
romance world. She took the concept of
"there are no bad ideas" and really ran with
it.

Thea Masen

Thea Masen never thought she'd write spicy romance. The first time she read a steamy book, she was so embarrassed she couldn't finish it. Now, she spends her days hiding her computer screen from her teenagers and her nights reading tantalizing snippets to her husband.

If you want sweet and spicy love stories, with a touch of the magical and imagined, you've come to the right place.

Unfortunate Reads

Cassie is an ADHD millennial mom of one from Baltimore who loves craft beer and chaos. Though she runs the Unfortunate Reads page, she reads and enjoys more than just the absolutely unhinged stories. She likes her books extra spicy, with a special fondness for PNR, Sci/fi, and Why Choose romance.

Cassie is a sex positive, feminist, LGBTQIA+ ally who supports indie authors and human artists. She loves to interact

with the bookstagram/booktok communities. There is no room for disparagement of books, authors, or readers on her pages. Reading is reading!
She began publishing in 2024, and quickly caught the writing bug. She is also a narrator and generally can't pick one facet of the book world to stay in.

Vera Valentine
An unapologetic book-huffer and devourer-of-stories, **Vera Valentine** has carried on a torrid love affair with the written word for nearly all of her 40 years. Grown in the diner-laden wilds of the New Jersey Pine Barrens and transplanted to North Carolina, she lives with her husband, eight cats, and two dogs, most of whom are house trained. An avid fan of the Paranormal 'Why Choose?' / Queer Polyam genre, she initially tossed her author hat into the ring in September of 2021. Since then, she's applied her pen to more than a dozen books full of spicy romance, angst, and dry humor, including fear-feeding cryp-

tids, Easter bunny aliens, and omegaverse balloon animal shifters.

A self-professed chaotic capybara, Vera can usually be found spending too much time on social media, chilling with fellow authors, or scribbling down plot bunny ideas in her trusty paper sidekick, the Bad Idea Book™.

If you'd like to stay in touch and up-to-date on Vera's latest projects, pop by www.ValentineVerse.com to follow her on social media, sign up for the Valentin-eVerse Newsletter, and more! :)